Dear Parents:

Congratulations! Your child is taking the first steps on an exciting journey. The destination? Independent reading!

STEP INTO READING® will help your child get there. The program offers five steps to reading success. Each step includes fun stories and colorful art or photographs. In addition to original fiction and books with favorite characters, there are Step into Reading Non-Fiction Readers, Phonics Readers and Boxed Sets, Sticker Readers, and Comic Readers—a complete literacy program with something to interest every child.

Learning to Read, Step by Step!

Ready to Read   Preschool–Kindergarten
• big type and easy words • rhyme and rhythm • picture clues
For children who know the alphabet and are eager to begin reading.

Reading with Help   Preschool–Grade 1
• basic vocabulary • short sentences • simple stories
For children who recognize familiar words and sound out new words with help.

Reading on Your Own   Grades 1–3
• engaging characters • easy-to-follow plots • popular topics
For children who are ready to read on their own.

Reading Paragraphs   Grades 2–3
• challenging vocabulary • short paragraphs • exciting stories
For newly independent readers who read simple sentences with confidence.

Ready for Chapters   Grades 2–4
• chapters • longer paragraphs • full-color art
For children who want to take the plunge into chapter books but still like colorful pictures.

STEP INTO READING® is designed to give every child a successful reading experience. The grade levels are only guides; children will progress through the steps at their own speed, developing confidence in their reading.

Remember, a lifetime love of reading starts with a single step!

Visit us on the Web!
StepIntoReading.com
randomhousekids.com

Educators and librarians, for a variety of teaching tools, visit us at RHTeachersLibrarians.com

ISBN 978-0-399-55886-3 (trade) — ISBN 978-0-399-55887-0 (lib. bdg.)

Printed in the United States of America

10 9 8 7 6 5 4

nickelodeon.

Shimmer and Shine™

Magical Mermaids!

based on the teleplay "Mermaid Mayhem"
by Brian Swenlin and Jennifer Bardekoff

illustrated by Dave Aikins

Random House 🏠 New York

Shimmer and Shine dress
Tala like a mermaid.

Leah has three wishes.
She wishes to see
a real mermaid.

First wish of the day!
Leah is on a boat
to Enchanted Falls.

Leah, Shimmer, and
Shine meet Nila.
She is a real mermaid!

Nila dives into the water.

Leah wishes she
could follow Nila.

Second wish of the day!
Leah, Shimmer, and Shine
are mermaids!

Nila juggles bubbles!

Third wish of the day!
Now Leah can
juggle bubbles, too.

Oh, no!

Leah is out of wishes.

How will they get home?

The Mermaid Gem
will help—
if they can get it.
It is protected
by a sea monster!

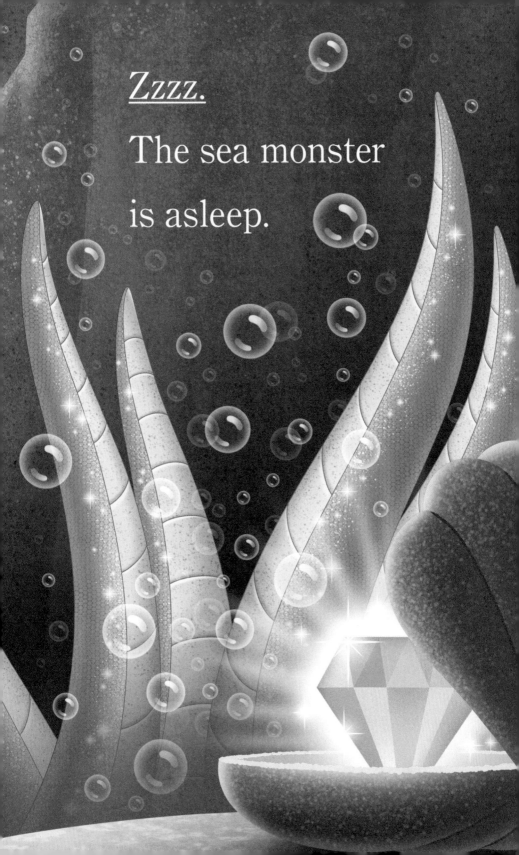

Zzzz.

The sea monster
is asleep.

Oops!
Shine wakes
the sea monster!

The sea monster
will not share the Gem.

If the Gem is gone, who will visit the dark cave?

Leah, the genies, and Nila
promise to visit.

Shimmer makes
shiny stars
to light up the cave.

Now the cave is not dark!

The sea monster is happy.

She shares the Gem.

Poof!

The Mermaid Gem sends
the friends to their boat.
With the Gem,
they can visit anytime!